PATRICK JONES

darbycreek

MINNEAPOLIS

Darby Creek
A division of Lerner Publishing Group, Inc.
241 First Avenue North
Minneapolis, MN 55401 USA

For reading levels and more information, look up this title at www.lernerbooks.com.

Front cover: © choreograph/123RF.com (rose); © iStockphoto.com/pzRomashka (smoke background).

Main body text set in Janson Text LT Std 12/17.5.
Typeface provided by Adobe Systems.

Library of Congress Cataloging-in-Publication Data

The Cataloging-in-Publication Data for *Heart or Mind* is on file at the Library of Congress.
ISBN 978-1-5124-0003-8 (LB)
ISBN 978-1-5124-0091-5 (PB)
ISBN 978-1-5124-0092-2 (eb PDF)

Manufactured in the United States of America
1 – SB – 12/31/15

To Ali, Chioma, Nasteho, Olivia,
and Sabrina
—P.J.

1

RODNEY

"Abdi Warsame, Abdi Ali," Marquese says in a monotone. "Abdi Omar, Abdi Aynte, Abdi—"

"You're losing it. Whatcha doing?" Rodney asks as he, Marquese, and Bryant enter the cafeteria.

"I'm countin' Somalis," Marquese says, then points across the crowded room at Minneapolis's Northeast High. Bryant, a former football teammate of Rodney's, snorts like a pig with laughter. Rodney puts in his earbuds to drown out Marquese's nonstop blathering and the roar of a room housing twice its hundred-student capacity. After the silence of too many nights in a CIU cell, the packed cafeteria seems louder than the school's football games. No matter, Rodney has eyes for only two: his ex, Aaliyah, and her new boy, Antonio. She dumped Rodney by letter when he was doing time at County Home School.

"Bro, that's racist," Rodney snaps at Marquese. "I mean, given some of the—"

"Listen Rod, it ain't like it was before you went inside." Marquese speaks to Rodney but never takes his eyes off of the assembly of tall, thin, and neatly dressed Somali teen boys. Like most Minneapolis schools, Northeast's diversity isn't about black and white but about kids of many different colors. The only colors lacking at Northeast are green and gold—the colors of money.

"The Somalis are taking over our turf," Marquese continues.

Rodney says nothing. Like Marquese, Rodney spent many an hour standing on a street corner, sometimes making more in a week than his mom did in a month. But that was before his six month placement at the CHS (County Home School) spent STAMPing (Short Term Adolescent Male Program) and doing CBT (Cognitive Behavioral Therapy), which at the start seemed like real BS. A lot of letters, but it turned out OK.

"Somebody's gotta take 'em down before we lose all our business. Get me, Rodney?" Marquese asks.

"It ain't gonna be me," Rodney answers as they get in line for food. Rodney's never been into hating for the sake of hating. He cares about his mom and his friends, but mostly about getting Aaliyah back. Hating wastes his time. "I got other stuff to do."

"Not playing football," Bryant says, before stuffing his mouth with fries covered with bacon and cheese. Bryant wears a Northeast High letter jacket like the one Rodney used to wear.

"I've got to study." Rodney slams his heavy book bag off Bryant's shoulder.

"You ain't wearing the purple and white of the team and—" Bryant starts.

Marquese cuts him off. "Or ATK colors. Rodney, you ain't even black, you acting white."

Rodney feels his face flush with the toxic combination of humiliation and irritation. Beneath his dark black skin, his cheeks grow red. "I thought you guys were my friends. I thought you—"

Then it happens. In the center of the cafeteria, the two rival groups smash together like atoms in the supercollider Rodney hopes to study in college. It starts with Devonte and his crew jawing loudly with Farhan and his crew: the descendants of slaves versus the offspring of Somali war refugees.

Rodney freezes as a roar drowns the room like a tidal wave. He won't fight. He watches first the talking, then the yelling, and then the shoving. Next comes food flying, and then comes fists being thrown. A normal loud lunch hour turns to a manic war zone in minutes. *Trouble*, Rodney thinks, *follows me like a rumor.*

Somali boys rage against black boys. Kids

from the other groups—Latinos and whites and some of the girls who aren't in the fight—watch from the sidelines. Some laugh, some take cover behind tables, some run for the exit.

Teachers run for help, for safety, for their lives. The security guards near the door are yelling into their walkie-talkies and motioning to each other.

Food and punches fly, and cafeteria knives are wielded like weapons.

Marquese picks up Bryant's tray filled with bacon-covered fries and hurls them in the direction of a group of charging Somali young men. "Eat pork!" Marquese yells.

In response, one of the Somali students, a thin but hard-looking boy, hurls a saltshaker at Marquese.

Marquese ducks, and the saltshaker sails past. Rodney hits the floor. Behind him, he hears a clank and then a yelp, like someone who's been kicked. He turns and sees a Somali girl in a long grayish dress but with one of those white head scarves. She's lying on the filthy floor. Another Somali girl crawls to the girl's aid. From the corner of his eye, Rodney sees the fight coming toward the Somali girls. Teachers drop back; gang girls surge forward.

A group of four black girls starts toward the two Somali girls, who seek shelter under a table on the dirty cafeteria floor. Rodney hears their muffled crying. Turning his back to the mob, Rodney bends down. "Are you okay?" he asks the wounded girl. That girl says nothing, while the other, wearing broken glasses and a hearing aid, stares lightning bolts at him. "Is she okay?" Rodney asks the girl with glasses.

"Let's kick their—" a girl starts to yell, but she's cut off by a roar of crowd voices. Rodney looks at the girl on the floor and then up at the charging crowd. He can see that one of girls in the crowd, well under five feet tall, displays a knife.

"Back off!" Rodney yells as he positions himself between the crowd and the girl. Her white scarf is soiled with drops of blood. "Don't mess with them or me. Hear me?"

The girls turn away, not so much afraid as irritated, Rodney thinks. They start toward another group of Somali girls. Chairs, books, and anything else not nailed down sail across the room like a zero-gravity space chamber. Rodney sees Farhan and Devonte in a UFC-style brawl on the top of a table. One of the teachers trips an alarm, which only adds to the panic in the room.

"The police have been called!" a voice booms over a loudspeaker, but everybody seems unmoved by words, only motivated by actions. It's hard to tell which kids started the fight, because the entire cafeteria seems in motion. Everyday cafeteria items fly through the air or are brandished as assault weapons.

"Are you okay?" Rodney yells to the Somali girl on the floor holding her head. "Let me see." She takes off the scarf, and Rodney sees the big cut on her forehead from where the saltshaker smashed into her flawless face.

The girl nods and blinks her soft brown eyes, the corners of her mouth forming a hurt smile.

"You need to move! Run to the door!" Rodney tells her. "Can you move?"

The girl tries to say something but then clutches her forehead and passes out, face first on the floor. With debris flying over him, Rodney turns the girl to face him. Amid the chaos of the cafeteria and beneath the ruckus of the riot, Rodney grows light-headed and feels his heart race.

He's felt this twice before: once in ninth grade when he got shot, and again in tenth grade when he fell in love with Aaliyah. Rodney pulls the girl's head closer to him and the feeling grows deeper. Stronger.

The lights of the cafeteria turn off and on, but Rodney can see glowing spots like a thousand fireflies from cell phones videoing the melee. Rodney covers his face; his PO won't like this.

"You're safe with me," Rodney tells the unconscious girl. In the cafeteria, the October armageddon continues, but holding the wounded young Somali girl in his arms, Rodney has never felt safer. Stronger. Better.

JAWAHIR

"Get your thug hands off her," Ayaan yells at the young man shielding Jawahir.

"I'm protecting her," the guy says softly. His mouth is almost against Jawahir's left ear. Jawahir's eyes open again, but she can't make words come from her throat. She thinks he smells nice, not loaded with rank cologne to cover the stink of cigarettes or weed like so many boys at Northeast.

"We protect our own," Ayaan says. Jawahir

hears a thump. The young man grunts in pain, no doubt from her cousin's kick. "Get back to your corner selling poison, killing your community, and—"

"Listen, I don't want to hear—" the young man starts to speak, but he stops as Farhan, Abdi Ali, and Ayub pounce, fists and kicks flying. He makes no noise, but the others shout curses in Somali.

"Stop!" Jawahir cries out, but the boys don't listen. She tries again. "Please stop!"

"He jumped her," Ayaan shouts at the attacking boys. "I saw it."

"No, that's not what—" Jawahir starts to speak, but bodies tumble around her as a group of black students, one of them wearing a varsity jacket, comes to help the person who came to her aid. She thinks about her mom's stories about the homeland, when she felt helpless as young men waged war in front of her.

Jawahir tries to regain her feet and crawl to safety, but stumbles. She covers her head with her hands and feels the hot blood oozing. She knows her hijab is ruined; her dad will be angry.

"Follow me," Jawahir hears the boy mumble. He rises to his hands and knees, head down. She sees the blood dripping from his head. The young man reaches his hands underneath Jawahir's arms and pulls her to safety under a table. The floor is slippery with spilled food, drink puddles, and specks of blood.

The riot continues until the doors burst open and a squad of police with clubs, helmets, and shields pushes through the crowd. Jawahir starts to speak to the young man, but he's ripped from under the table. Along with other black students, he stands by police order with his hands up, casual, as if out of habit.

RODNEY

"Okay, who started this?" Principal Evans asks the group of bloodied African American teen boys who are lined up against the wall of the cafeteria. Evans is an older white woman with frizzy short gray hair. She wears an orange, pink, and green dress she must have bought in her hippie days.

Minneapolis police in riot gear stand behind her and tower over her. It's just Rodney and his friends lined up: the Somali boys were taken to another room, and Rodney didn't see any girls detained. *Too bad*, Rodney thinks. *I want to see that girl again.*

"Basically, I need to know what happened," the principal continues.

A school nurse hands out towels to wipe away the blood and Band-Aids to cover the cuts. "You have violated, literally, multiple rules laid out in our student handbook, to say nothing of the law." Evans nods toward the police officers as she says this. Rodney says nothing. Evans quotes the handbook as if it's the Bible. But the student handbook is only the third most important set of rules to follow: first comes the code of the streets and then the police law that lands you inside. "Really, no one is talking?"

The police officers, irritated with their silence, get more aggressive. A few start in-your-face questioning. The old white guy in blue spitting questions at Rodney must have had Taco Bell for lunch. He reeks of meat.

"The woman asked you a question," the officer says. "Who did that to you?"

The officer's finger almost touches the cut on Rodney's forehead. It will need stiches. He thought he was past police encounters, but it seems history always repeats itself with kids at Northeast.

"You deaf?"

Rodney stays silent. The police have a code, known as the blue wall, but so do the streets: you don't snitch on your friends, or your enemies.

"Well, here's the deal. My guess is more than one of you is on probation, parole, or EHM, so being in this brawl violates that. You tell us what happened here or you'll spend homecoming night at JDC. Talk, you walk. Everybody understand?"

Marquese starts laughing, and most everyone else follows suit. Rodney bites his bottom lip so hard that blood dribbles down his chin. "Actually, nothing about this is funny," Evans says.

"Ally, she's the riot," Marquese whispers to Rodney on his left, then Bryant on his right. They call Evans "Ally" because she uses the words *actually*, *basically*, *really*, and *literally* all the time.

Evans keeps talking, but Rodney and the others don't listen until she says, "Zero tolerance. That means, gentlemen, all of you are suspended for violating the student code—"

"Excuse me, Principal Evans, a word," football coach Martin says. Other than the whistle around his neck, Coach Martin looks, and sounds, a lot like the cops. Rodney and the others stand silently under the angry gaze of the police. Rodney scans the crowd: he's had run-ins with more than one of these blue suits before. He doesn't want to get violated. It's like real-life Monopoly: he'd go directly to jail. *It's not fair*, Rodney thinks, *but few things are fair about life in North Minneapolis.*

"Bryant, Antonio, Rasheed." Coach Martin starts calling off the names of the football players and directs them toward the open cafeteria door.

Bryant looks at Rodney, shrugs his shoulders, and smiles. "Could have been you, bro," he whispers to Rodney and then joins his teammates by the door. Once they're all assembled, Coach Martin leads them outside. They'll avoid the inside, it seems.

"Now, we literally have a zero-tolerance policy," Evans says. "So the next time—"

Evans keeps talking, but Rodney tunes her out. Next time. Another chance. Another chance to talk to Aaliyah. Another chance to see the Somali girl he helped and who, in just one look, bumped his heart. He's felt nothing but guilt in his life; she seems nothing but innocent.

"So, do all of you basically understand? This is over," Evans says.

Marquese jabs Rodney in the ribs with his elbow. "Ally's wrong, actually," Marquese whispers. "This is literally just getting started." Rodney winces, the promised threat more painful than the poke.

4

"I'm going to sue the school!" Jawahir's dad shouts. She's unclear, as always, if her dad is talking to her or through his Bluetooth to the person on the other end of the call. They're in the family's van driving home from school. Ayaan sits in back next to Jawahir, her left hand holding Jawahir's hand while her right scrolls through the Twitterstorm about a food fight now being called a race riot.

"I have a headache," Jawahir whispers,

knowing she'd have to scream to be heard over Dad's ranting as he switches between English and Somali. It's clear that her father's not letting this go. Jawahir figures out that her dad's talking to Ahmeed Hassan, his best friend and business partner, as well as Farhan's father. And when, not if, the two dads get their way, Ahmeed will be Jawahir's father-in-law.

"Did you see Farhan fighting?" Ayaan whispers. "He looked so brave and strong."

Jawahir nods, but she thinks the boy who came to her aid acted much braver. That the short-fuse Farhan would fight doesn't surprise Jawahir. She knows her cousin has a crush on Farhan, and Ayaan's not the only one.

"We should pull them out of that school," Jawahir's father says. "Start our own school to teach the next generation the right values and keep them away from those—"

Whenever her father talks about the African American boys at her school, Jawahir wishes she wore a hearing aid like Ayaan so she could turn it off and be deaf to his hateful words.

"Hey look, it's us!" Ayaan shouts. She thrusts her phone in Jawahir's direction. Somebody's posted footage of the fight on YouTube. Jawahir can see the brawl in the background, but whoever shot the video focused on Jawahir, Ayaan, and the boy who helped her.

"Do you know him?" Jawahir whispers, embarrassed at what she's feeling. It's not just that she needs to thank him, but she also wants to see him again. A longing feeling growls in her belly like a hunger while fasting.

"Serious?" Ayaan answers. "One good deed doesn't mean he's not one of them."

"But I thought—" Jawahir starts, but it's hard to talk over her dad's shouts and under the "don't think about it" stare from Ayaan. *I'm not thinking for once*, Jawahir whispers to herself, *I'm feeling.*

5

RODNEY

"So, that's basically what I'd like to do," Principal Evans says. She has gathered a small group of students into the media center after school to participate in a "healing effort" in response to the riot. Rodney's unsure why he was asked there; he's a follower, not a leader. That didn't change in six months. Marquese, a real leader, was not invited and is plotting revenge.

Two white security guards and one even whiter police officer stand next Evans. Outside the library in the halls of Northeast, those numbers are way higher. Two days have passed since the riot, and tensions remain high.

"Are there questions?" Evans asks.

ZamZam, one of the Somali girls invited to the meeting, raises her hand. Rodney wants to question her, though: *Do you know the girl that I helped?* But he says nothing. Instead, he's focusing on his knock-off Chucks, trying not to look at Aaliyah. Not her model pretty face, not her hand intertwined with Antonio's ugly hand. After Aliyah dumped him, Antonio pounced on her quicker than he ever did any fumble. Defensive end on the field, but an offensive jerk in Rodney's eyes.

"So let me introduce the two community leaders who will actually lead the effort to help us heal," Principal Evans says. "This is Reverend Elijah Cook from the Bethel AME Church and Shaykh Abdi Abdallah from the Imaam Shaafici Mosque. With them, we will basically . . ."

Rodney shuts out the rest of the meeting; he doesn't want to be there. He has other things to do after school, namely a meeting with his probation officer, Mr. Burton. Burton has been buzzing Rodney's phone all day, no doubt to remind him of their meeting.

"What's going on, all?" Marquese shouts as he throws open the door of the media center, quite uninvited. Principal Evans summons one of the guards toward the door. "You meeting without me?"

"Marquese, you were not invited to this meeting, but—"

"You invite him but not me?" Marquese points at Farhan, who sits in the chair nearest Evans. "Rodney, you don't want to be sitting down with them."

Rodney looks at his best friend, then back at the principal. Farhan stares him down.

"Rodney was invited to this meeting, you were not. You need to leave!" Evans directs the one of the security officers to remove Marquese, who loudly protests the entire way. During the commotion, Rodney peeks at his phone, heavy with missed messages and texts. He wonders if somebody died.

After Marquese leaves, the holy men talk about healing, but Rodney thinks it's all rote, kind of like the stuff his PO says. Stuff Burton's got to say, but deep down probably he doesn't really believe. Burton, like some other POs Rodney's had, used to be in "the game" but got out and is now on the other side. It seems to Rodney, though, that Burton's more interested in telling war stories than anything else.

"So, basically, we'll meet until we get this resolved," Evans says. Rodney steals another glance at his phone, thinking that if it had a weather app, he'd look to see if hell was freezing over anytime soon.

Rodney gets up to leave with everyone else, but Principal Evans calls him to the front.

"Rodney, I want to thank you—" Evans starts.

"Why me?" Rodney asks aloud what he'd been thinking since he got asked to the meeting.

"Because you set an example protecting those girls." Evans sounds proud, like she did something.

"How do you know about that?"

She shakes her head, surprised. She pulls her out her crappy old phone and shows him a video posted on YouTube of him protecting the girl during the riot. "The district is trying to get these videos of the incident pulled down, but I guess it has literally—what is it you all say—gone viral."

"Who is the girl?" Rodney asks, trying to appear all calm and casual.

"I know the girl in the glasses is Ayaan Farrah," Evans says. "I can't see the other girl's face. I invited Ayaan to the meeting, but she declined. I'm sure that girl will find you—"

Rodney bolts from the room thinking, *not if I find her first*.

6

JAWAHIR

"Why would I want to go to some stupid meeting?" Ayaan asks Jawahir just before the start of first period the next morning. *Because I bet he was invited*, Jawahir thinks to herself, but says nothing.

"Farhan said he'd handle things for us," Ayaan continues. "But I think it's a bad idea for him to be sitting around with all those thugs."

"That's not a very nice thing to say," Jawahir counters as the second bell rings. A wave of students hurries through the door and takes their usual seats. Some of the Somali kids Jawahir and Ayaan know fill the seats around them. Jawahir notices that the African American kids are sitting together on the opposite side of the room.

It takes five minutes for Mr. Grayson to get the class quiet and another ten to explain the lab assignment. He ends with an announcement that he's assigned new lab partners. There are audible groans as he starts to read off the names. He's mixing it up—no way Jawahir will get to stay with Ayaan.

At the announcement of her lab partner, Jawahir reluctantly takes the seat next to Roshanda at the lab table. Roshanda is wearing designer clothes and lots of jewelry. Jawahir self-consciously touches her plain-colored hijab and starts counting down the minutes to the end of class.

Roshanda is texting instead of listening to the assignment, so Jawahir takes notes. She does 80 percent of the work but gets only 50 percent of the credit. It reminds her of her own household, with her mom working two jobs and raising her and her younger brothers.

"Is that you?" Roshanda asks, shoving her phone in Jawahir's face. It's the video of the brawl. "Who is that brother helping you?" Roshanda asks.

I'd love to know, Jawahir thinks. Jawahir asks for Roshanda to play the video again as she wonders, *Is love at first sight a chemical reaction?*

"Put that away Roshanda," Mr. Grayson snaps at her, like he does every day. She complies until the moment that he's out of sight, then she pulls it out again and shows Jawahir the video for a third time.

"You don't know him either?" Jawahir whispers. Hopes.

"Why, you think we're all related or something? Or maybe we all just look alike to you."

"That's not what I mean. I wanted to thank him, that's all." Jawahir realizes she could record in her lab notebook that today she had her longest conversation ever with Roshanda.

"You'd better hurry up, then, 'cause some brothers don't think what he did was cool at all."

"Where would I find him?" Jawahir asks, even softer.

"For serious?" Roshanda laughs, earning a scowl from the teacher. Mr. Grayson motions for her to close up her phone. Roshanda smiles, puts her phone face-up on the table.

"Yes."

"I heard he's a junior, so all depends what group he's with," Roshanda says, then explains where various groups congregate. Since Jawahir's father forbade her to reenter the cafeteria for fear of her safety if another riot breaks out, Jawahir can't visit the place she'd met the mystery man. Roshanda ends talking about the "nerds and nice boys" hanging out in the media center at lunch and after school.

He's got to be one of those, Jawahir thinks. She finishes the lab while Roshanda texts.

"But if I was you, I wouldn't be hanging around even nice boys. Best you stay with your kind, and we stay with ours. Know what I'm saying?" Jawahir cannot imagine a person in the universe more different from her father than Roshanda Tate, so how is it, she wonders, that they could think so much alike?

"Thanks for the advice," Jawahir says, trying to hide the ill-fitting sarcasm in her voice.

"It isn't advice," Roshanda laughs too loud, and then stares down Jawahir. "It is a warning."

7

RODNEY

"Rodney, I don't want to talk with you no more about this," Aaliyah says. Rodney waited until the end of the school day when he knew Antonio would head straight to football practice. He's got Aaliyah cornered near her locker. No one else is around. "I told you everything in that letter."

"That was cold, breaking up with me in a letter when I was inside," Rodney says.

"It was only a matter of time."

"Before we broke up?"

"No, before you got popped." She pushes Rodney hard in the chest, but he doesn't flinch.

"First off, I ain't like that no more." Rodney leans in, his face against hers. "And second, you used to like that about me. You didn't think nothing about it when I was buying you all kinds of—"

"Just a bunch of boys thinking they're men," Aaliyah mumbles. "I got no time for it now."

"And somehow Antonio is—"

"You ain't listening! This ain't about him, and it ain't even about you." Aaliyah begins to tear up. Rodney wonders if she's faking. "This is about the person I want to be, who I want to be with. It ain't you."

"I told you, I've changed. Ask around."

"Well, I saw that thing with the Somali chick, but one good deed don't—"

"It's not just one good deed, it's who I am."

Aaliyah laughs, not in a tone suggesting something's funny, but something's stupid. "You know why brothers like you and

Marquese do all that thug nonsense?"

Rodney stares at Aaliyah. He thinks it's wrong that she won't believe that he's changed. "Same reason fish swim. It's what they do."

Rodney's been punched, kicked, and even shot, but these words hurt worse. He drops his arms, backs up, and lets Aaliyah free.

Rodney stands tall, even though he feels like he just picked himself off the floor. He gathers his books and heads for the media center to study. He's got a future too, one without Aaliyah. Now that he's seen who she really is and what she really thinks, Rodney feels like a dark cloud just lifted from his sky.

8

JAWAHIR

"That's him," Jawahir whispers to Ayaan when she sees the young man walk into the library. Her body feels like it's short-circuiting, every sense overloading with new sensations. "That's him. That's the boy—"

"Sit down, girl!" Ayaan grabs her hand as Jawahir starts to stand and pulls her down. Ayaan sighs. "Jawahir, I see that look in your eyes. Don't do it. What is wrong with you? If your dad—"

"I just want—" Jawahir stops, stumbling over the unfamiliar word *want*. In her house, you did what you were told and what was needed. "Want" was as foreign and forbidden as pork or alcohol.

"Not just your dad," Ayaan says. "If Farhan or his friends see you even talk to him, they'll—"

Jawahir nods in agreement, smiles at her cousin politely, and frees herself from her grip. She walks quickly toward the door. Ayaan yells at her in Somali. Jawahir turns to see that the other girls at her table, and the boys at the adjoining tables, are staring at her. Some start texting.

The commotion gets the boy's attention. He stares at Jawahir, and a smile lights up his face. He starts toward her, walking and then almost running. "Fool, what are you doing?" someone yells from the door. Jawahir recognizes him from the video. He was the one fighting with Farhan on the table. Jawahir's rescuer stops, turns and stares at the other boy, but says nothing.

"I said, what are you doing?" the young man repeats. He's blocking the door. The first shout gets the attention of the other students in the room. Now everyone is staring at Jawahir. Some of the African American girls start shouting, but it's hard to hear because the Somali boys are shouting louder.

"I'm free. Screw this," the young man says. He reaches out his hand. Jawahir takes it. He drops his books on the floor and starts running toward the fire exit. Jawahir, hand in hand, follows. As he kicks the door open, a loud siren screams and lights flash. Jawahir lets go of his hand, and they sprint together toward the bus garage. The young man runs beside her. The sirens in the distance grow faint, and the sound of their breathing gets heavier as they reach the garage. "Let's stop running," he whispers.

The boy leans against the garage. Jawahir stands on her toes to kiss him. She feels ten feet tall.

RODNEY

"You are seriously messed up in the head," Marquese tells Rodney, who is tired of listening but is trapped with him on the light rail. "I think inside CHS they shrunk your skull and brain along with it."

"I don't want to hear it," Rodney finally says, shutting down the Marquese tirade. They are headed to the downtown library on a Saturday afternoon, Marquese to deal, Rodney to study. Not to study for school, but to study everything Rodney can about Jawahir, who plans to meet him there.

"I'm not one to say anything against a brother getting a little something," Marquese says. Rodney hates his tone; the idea of "getting a little something" seems vulgar even though not that long ago, that's how he thought and spoke. But about Jawahir, it just seems wrong. "But with all the crap since the fight. You representing all of us, so you're making us look bad falling for a Muslim."

"I can't explain." Rodney stares out the window as the train moves almost as slow as a city bus. He wants the train to move faster, but the only place the train picks up speed is out of the tunnel at the airport.

"You watch yourself 'cause the word is out, and they're just as pissed about that scene in the media center as us. Now, at the big library, first floor is neutral, we got the second, they got third. Be careful."

Rodney frowns at the idea of a library divided up like a war zone or like his neighborhood. Marquese keeps talking, and

Rodney pretends to listen, but he's thinking about Jawahir. They kissed before they knew each other's names, which seemed right to Rodney. Names are labels, and to Rodney, he thinks the world has too many labels, tats, and flags. Symbols used for war, not love.

Just before they split up in the library foyer, Marquese gives Rodney a fist bump. "Look, I'm just watching out for you. Times is tight now. You got to get your—"

"I love her."

Marquese's laughter bounces off the glass ceiling. "You just met her. You ain't even—"

"That's how I know, Marquese," Rodney explains. He's talking slow, making sure that his friend understands every word. "I shouldn't feel like this about some girl, some girl I don't know, some girl that everybody tells me to stay away from, but I can't. It's not just that she's beautiful, but she's something innocent and I ain't felt that way in a long time. This is real, not like Aaliyah who—"

"You're just rebounding from Aaliyah, that's all."

"No, you're not listening, Marquese. It's not like that. It's not a lie or a pose. This is real."

"Well, crap's going to get real, so whatever you gotta do, do it, but don't tell me. You hear me?"

Rodney smiles and bumps Marquese's fist. His thick knuckles are tough. Rodney remembers how small and soft Jawahir's hands were. Rodney's knees buckle with the memory of Jawahir's lips.

Marquese heads up the stairs to do business, while Rodney waits. Rodney wishes he could call Jawahir, but he knows her dad won't let her have a phone. Or Instagram, anything. She's doing nothing ordinary for a ninth-grade girl. It fits, he thinks, since she's extraordinary in every way. He'll have to wait until he sees her.

Finally, he hears footsteps approaching from behind him and spins around to see Jawahir approaching. But Jawahir's not alone. One of the tough Somali boys, Farhan, is with her. So is the mean girl Ayaan, who sneers at

Rodney from a distance. Rodney's ready to text Marquese for reenforcements.

"Stay away from her, thug," Farhan hisses like steam coming from the radiators in Rodney's old house. "I hear you talk to her again, let alone touch her, you answer to all of us. She belongs to me."

Rodney's hands dive into his pockets: phone in left ready to text; fist in right ready to fly.

"I'm sorry," Jawahir whispers as she passes by Rodney, following two steps behind Farhan, one behind Ayaan. Steps behind so neither see her toss a crumbled piece of paper behind her back. Rodney picks up the paper and smoothes it, reading words that fill his heart with joy. "Light rail station @ 2:00."

10

JAWAHIR

"Rodney, sit behind me," Jawahir whispers
to Rodney just before boarding the light rail.
Groups of Somali and black teens also board
the southbound train toward the airport. The
sunlight shines on her face. She sits facing the
Somali group, her back to Rodney. They stay
silent until the train starts moving. "Rodney,
can you hear me?" Jawahir whispers. She puts
a book in front of her face so no one can see
her talking, not that anyone seems to be paying

attention to her. She doesn't recognize any of the kids on the train, but she wonders if their mad dash the other day, like the brawl, is all the rage online.

"Why here? Is this really safe?" Rodney asks, softly.

"No place is safe for us, not school, not the library, not our neighborhoods."

"I don't know what I did," Rodney says. "That girl Ayaan gave me a look like—"

"My cousin doesn't like you."

"You know why? 'Cause she's jealous of you: of your beauty, of someone loving you like I do."

Jawahir notices her hands shaking. Did he really just say that he loved her? She wants to tell him the same, but even though meeting was her idea, now she's scared: not of Rodney, but of herself and a flood of feelings crashing like waves on some island beach. She's drowning in an ocean of emotion.

"Jawahir, say something," Rodney says, but Jawahir can't connect her heart to her throat to her lips. "I wish I could turn around and look at you. Get lost in your eyes."

More young people climb on the train at the Downtown East stop. More noise to cover their voices. When the train starts again, Rodney whispers, "I looked up your name. It means jewel. And you are that, Jawahir, a jewel: precious, something rare and too beautiful for this world. I want you."

"If only it was so easy," Jawahir whispers. "If we were some other place, some other time . . . I'd give up myself, my faith, my family for you. Is this crazy? Would you do the same for me?"

"I would do anything."

"Our skin color is the same. Why doesn't anyone else see that?" Jawahir unloads thoughts racing through her head. "And skin color shouldn't even matter, it's about blood. Your blood is red, my blood is red. It wouldn't matter to me if your skin was green or purple, you'd still be you underneath."

Rodney starts to speak, but at the Franklin stop the train fills mainly with older Somali women and young kids. Jawahir sees the women clutch their children and purses when they walk past her, no doubt because the only seats left on the train are where Rodney and other young black men are seated.

"This was a bad idea, Rodney," Jawahir whispers. "Maybe it's best if we—"

"I'm like this train, Jawahir. I may stop, but I will get where I'm going. And where I'm going is to you. Screw this, I'm going to turn around, sit next to you. This is stupid and—"

"No, it's a mistake, somebody will hurt you."

"It's worse being this close to you but not being able to see you, touch you, kiss you."

"Don't say that." Tension rises in Jawahir's voice because she feels the same, but can't bring herself to say the words. She's afraid not of her family or her friends, but of her out-of-control heart.

"Farhan, his friends, Ayaan, bring 'em on. Not being able to be with you is worse than death. Just turn around and look at me, Jawahir."

Jawahir whispers, "No." He can't see her blushing and starting to cry. "Don't, please."

"Fine, I'll do anything you ask," Rodney says. "You need me to walk across hot coals,

I'll do it. I don't have much, but I'd risk it all if you just say the words. Jawahir, say that you love me."

Jawahir presses the book against her forehead and closes her eyes. "I want to, but it's too quick. It's like lightning that flashes and then disappears before you can say, that was lightning."

"Maybe it's lightning for you, but for me, my heart is thunder exploding out of my chest."

Jawahir rises as the train pulls into the Lake Street station. "I didn't expect you to say those words to me, Rodney. I need time. Tomorrow, after school, outside the garage. I will have my answer."

Rodney stands next to her. As the train stops, there's a slight jolt. Rodney presses up against Jawahir, she presses back. Her five senses overflow in the split second they touch.

"Love isn't an answer," Rodney whispers. "It's a promise. And I promise it to you."

11

RODNEY

"So that's the story, Larry," Rodney says. Rodney's uncle Larry sits across from him in a small apartment near the airport where Larry works. Larry didn't react as Rodney told him about Jawahir.

Larry smiles, but Rodney's not sure if he's happy for him or thinks he's a fool, and he's afraid to ask. Larry smokes, smiles, smokes, and keeps Rodney guessing. "So what do you think?" Rodney asks.

"Honest, Poe, I think you're making a big mistake," Larry says. He calls Rodney "Poe," short for poet. While all of Rodney's friends were writing raps in middle school, Rodney was writing poetry. The name didn't stick with his friends, but Larry adopted it. Rodney likes the name, but at this moment he hates his uncle's words.

"I'm sorry you think that. I thought you of anyone . . ." Rodney points to the picture of Larry's ex, Valentina. Her family was also members of a rival gang to the ATK.

"And how did that end up?" Larry inhales deeply, then puts out the smoke in the full ashtray.

"But that doesn't mean for me—"

"You came here, and I'm always glad to see you Poe, but you came here out of nowhere and told me this story about you and this Somali girl. I got friends. I know what's happening on the street. I heard about the fight at your school, everybody treating it like it was big news, but it ain't. This is old."

"You mean back in your day?" Rodney asks.

Larry is twice Rodney's age.

"Blacks and Somalis been going at it almost since day one," Larry says. "But if you study your history, you'll know that's just how it works in this country." While in prison, Larry earned a history degree from the university, although because of his own history, he'd never found a job where he could put it to use. Still, Larry is one of the most educated people Rodney knows.

"We should be on the same side."

"*Should* is way different from *are*," he says. "Besides, we got rival gangs in our own community who should be coming together, but instead they're tearing the north end apart. But like I said, it's old news."

"But maybe if Jawahir and I became a couple in public, maybe that would—"

"You ain't just a poet, Rodney, you're also a dreamer. This is the real world we live in."

Rodney says nothing. He sips the root beer his uncle gave him.

"Arabs and Jews, Sunni and Shia, Hatfields and McCoys, Bloods and Crips, forever wars."

"Why do people hate so much, Larry?" Rodney asks.

"Because hate is easier than love, and most people choose what's easy."

Rodney finishes his beverage, stands up from the small table, and walks toward the window. He looks at the airplanes taking off and landing. The window vibrates with their noise. "It's not a choice."

"What's that now?"

Rodney turns back to face Larry. "That's what nobody understands, I don't have a choice."

Larry laughs. "That's true for a young black man in—"

"No, that's not what I'm talking about, Larry." Rodney walks toward his uncle. He puts his hands on the table, leans in, smells the lingering smoke and his eyes start to water. "I don't have a choice about Jawahir. I know it's sudden and I know it's crazy, but I love her and want to be with her. I could no more choose not to want her than I could choose not to breathe. I could no more—"

Larry laughs and motions for Rodney to sit

back down. "Alright Poe, I hear you."

"Sorry, but I can't stop thinking about her. She's like a drug in my blood. You know?"

Larry nods. "So do you want my blessing, is that it?"

"And a place for us to—"

"I get you, Poe," Larry says. He scratches his shaved head, tugs on his ear.

"I have nowhere else," Rodney says. "And like I said, I don't have a choice."

Larry says nothing, deep in thought like the professor or teacher he wanted to be before the streets swallowed him up and then spit him into Stillwater State Prison for five years. "Like a drug, huh?"

"The kisses from Jawahir are the track marks on my heart."

Larry laughs loudly. "That's enough Poe, that's enough with the sweet stuff. I'll help you out."

"Thanks Larry."

"But I just want you to know something." Larry pulls out another cigarette with his right hand, picks up his lighter with his left.

He flicks the lighter but doesn't light the Salem 100. Instead he holds it in front of Rodney. "Rodney, love isn't a drug. It is a fire and it consumes everything in its path."

12

JAWAHIR

"Ayaan, you're family, that comes first," Jawahir whispers to her cousin. They're in her dad's van on the way to school. Since the brawl, her father has insisted on driving Jawahir, Ayaan, and Farhan to school each morning. Farhan sits in the passenger seat talking with Jawahir's father, acting like he's interested in her father's war stories about the homeland. Jawahir cares about nothing in the past, only about her future with Rodney.

"I don't approve," Ayaan responds, sensing what Jawahir is about to say. "You're blind to give up Farhan for that thug."

"I don't need your approval, I need your help," Jawahir whispers almost in a hiss. "We're family. We're supposed to be there for each other. I would do anything you asked me to do if only—"

"If you would do anything, then stop this nonsense with that thug who only has one thing—"

"He's not a thug, why do you say that? You don't even know him."

"I don't need to know him," Ayaan replies. "Open your eyes."

"I have open eyes, but also an open heart."

"An open heart's not all he wants."

Jawahir slaps her cousin's face.

"What is going on?" her father shouts from the front seat. Farhan turns toward the girls and breaks out what Jawahir thinks is a hundred-karat fake smile.

Jawahir stares at her cousin, whose eyes are starting to water. "Nothing. Right, Ayaan?"

Ayaan says nothing. For Jawahir it's a test of trust.

"Ayaan, you okay?" Farhan asks.

Ayaan nods and smiles back at Farhan. "Everything's fine."

"I'll pick you up right after school," Jawahir's father reminds everyone.

"Ayaan and I have to study for a test, right, Ayaan?" Jawahir says quickly, hoping the rush of words will cover up the lie. She's never lied to her father before; she never even imagined doing so.

"Right," Ayaan mumbles. Farhan looks confused, but turns back to Jawahir's father. Her father has started telling a new story about the honor and bravery of war, but Jawahir tunes him out. Her father lives in the past; she wants to live in the future. A future without war, a future filled with love. A future with Rodney.

13

"I thought you weren't coming," Rodney says to Jawahir as she joins him at the corner of the school parking garage. "I was worried you'd listen to what everyone's saying, decide it wasn't worth it."

"Don't say such a thing," Jawahir says.

"Look, I have a place." Rodney tells Jawahir about his visit with Uncle Larry, including Larry's warning about how love is like fire. Jawahir cools his talk of fire with a kiss. Rodney wants to say more, but he can't break away. With his back against the wall, Rodney breaks the kiss and pulls Jawahir tight to his chest. His heart beats louder than any bass. "Can you say the words? Will you make the promise?"

Jawahir stands on her toes to get her mouth even with his left ear. "I love you." She repeats the phrase over and over.

"Tomorrow night, we will—" Rodney starts.

"You'll do nothing," Farhan says. He stands six feet away. The rage in his normally steely green eyes burns like a molten lava. Ayaan is two feet behind him. "Take your hands off her."

Jawahir starts to back away, but Rodney pulls her even tighter.

"I said take your hands—"

Jawahir turns her head toward Farhan. "Farhan, this is none of your business."

Farhan takes a step closer. "You dishonor all of us. You betray your family."

Rodney leans down and whispers into Jawahir ear, "I love you. Run!" Rodney releases

Jawahir and takes off running away from school toward the street. Jawahir follows, with Farhan and Ayaan close behind. "This way!" Rodney shouts when Jawahir catches up. He grabs her hand and they run together.

They run hard against the wind, but Farhan and Ayaan are only steps behind. Rodney directs Jawahir toward a park a few blocks away from the school. A park he used to know well. As he'd hoped, when they arrive at the park, Marquese and a few others are mixing basketball and business.

"What the hell, bro?" Marquese yells when he sees Rodney and Jawahir. He bounces the ball in front of him as the two get closer to the court, but then he stops. Rodney and Jawahir reach Marquese and stop running. Rodney bends over and takes a deep breath, and then he sees Farhan. But behind him is no longer just Ayaan, but a small group of Somali young men. Most carry weapons they must have grabbed on the way: a piece of pipe, a broken bottle, and assorted other makeshift tools of destruction.

As Farhan and his group close, Marquese directs everyone to stand behind him. Rodney wonders if Marquese or any of the others are carrying.

"This is our park," Marquese yells at Farhan.

Farhan puts his hands in the air as if surrendering. "This isn't about turf. It's about them." Farhan points at Rodney and Jawahir, who stand directly behind Rodney, both breathing heavy.

"Truth is, I don't like it any more than you," Marquese says. "But he's blood, so—"

"This isn't between you and me." Farhan walks slowly toward Marquese. "It's between me and Rodney. He's taken something that was promised to me. He's soiled something innocent. He has—"

"Man, just shut up and get the hell out of my park."

Farhan cocks his head, gives Marquese a crazed look. "Not until we settle this."

"Settle what?"

Farhan takes off his jacket and lays it on

the ground. He takes a switchblade from his pocket and sets it on top of his jacket, then points at Rodney. "He wins, he keeps her. Except he won't."

Marquese turns to stare at Rodney, who isn't moving an inch other than to pull Jawahir closer to him. "No, I'm not fighting him," Rodney says to Marquese, shaking his head. "I'm not getting violated and going back inside. I'm not—"

"Where does all this fighting get us? It needs to end sometime. That time is now," Jawahir says.

"Looks like there ain't gonna be no fight," Marquese says, "so get your—"

But Farhan cuts him off with a string of slurs and swears directed at Rodney. "You best bounce," Marquese says, but Rodney pushes pass him. Jawahir tries to stop him, but Rodney steps forward.

"Come on, you heard her. Where does all this fighting get us? It needs to end sometime. That time is now," Rodney says. He imagines Jawahir smiling at him for using her words, but

Farhan isn't smiling. His sneer screams hate.

Rodney puts his hand behind him. "Jawahir, we're leaving, together." Jawahir steps forward, takes Rodney's hand and clutches it so hard that Rodney winces in pain. They start to leave, but Farhan stands in their way. Rodney says nothing and tries to step around him, but Farhan cuts him off.

"Just leave us alone."

Farhan answers by spitting in Rodney's face. Rodney wipes the spittle from his face onto Farhan's shirt. Farhan responds by pushing Rodney down. Jawahir throws herself on top of Rodney to protect him.

"Get out of the way!" Farhan shouts, but Jawahir won't budge. Farhan grabs her arm and pulls her up, pushes her away, and then balls his fists. He motions for Rodney to stand. Rodney stands, takes a deep breath, and stares at Farhan with an icy glare he learned on the streets, but Farhan doesn't blink.

Rodney looks back at Marquese and his friends, all of them yelling at him to fight, but then he gazes at Jawahir. She mouths the word "no."

Rodney reaches his hand toward Jawahir, but Farhan knocks it away. Three times, Rodney reaches his hand out, and three times Farhan chops it, each time harder. "You can do that a hundred times, Farhan, and the answer's the same. I'm not fighting you. This stupid war, for me, is over."

Farhan pushes Rodney's chest hard, backing him up until he's forced him against the fence. The two crowds of young men converge, but keep their distance. "A thousand times, Farhan, and I won't—"

"Screw this MLK crap!" Marquese steps forward. "You want to fight someone? Let's go!"

Farhan turns his back to Marquese and walks back toward his jacket, but he doesn't pick up the jacket, he picks up the blade. Rodney hears the blade come out and tries to get between Farhan and Marquese, but they're both charging forward. Farhan pushes the blade toward Rodney but misses. His hand goes underneath Rodney's arm and stabs Marquese in the chest. Marquese cries out in pain.

Rodney grabs Farhan's wrist and slams it against his knee. The bloody blade falls to the ground next to Marquese. Blood squirts from the wound in Marquese's chest. Still holding onto Farhan's wrist with his left hand, Rodney's right forms a fist that breaks Farhan's nose with the first blow, loosens his teeth with the second, and knocks him out with the third. Even as Farhan is falling toward the ground, Rodney keeps throwing punches until he hears Jawahir yell at him to stop. Her yelling seems louder than the rest of the shouts from the park, which has erupted into a brawl, but the sounds of police sirens soon drown all other noise.

14

"Back to back," Jawahir whispers as she and Rodney board the southbound train. Behind them, in the park, the brawl rages on. Farhan's and Marquese's injuries were the first, probably not the worst.

"Are you hurt?" Rodney asks. "Tell me you're okay." Jawahir's knees are scraped, but there's no blood. That's not true, she knows, for Rodney. His knuckles are bloody and his hand is probably broken.

"I'm fine," Jawahir lies. Love has consumed her ability to tell the truth. "Where are we going?"

"My uncle Larry's place," Rodney says. "We can hide out there until—" Rodney stops.

"Until what?" Jawahir asks, but there's silence between them even as the everyday sounds of light-rail commuters surround them. Jawahir doesn't know how to finish the sentence either.

"I'll call him," Rodney says. Jawahir stares ahead, her hands covering her mouth. No one looks at her or out the window, all of them focused on the two-by-three inches of screen in front of them.

Jawahir's heart beats so fast she feels like it is about to jump out of her chest and run away, and she knows that's the only answer: for her and Rodney to run away. She can't go back to school, back home, back to where everybody will have heard what Rodney did to Farhan. For a second, the fear of her future overwhelms Jawahir when she realizes she has nowhere to run, nowhere to turn, and nowhere to hide.

Sooner or later they'll have to get off the train.

"Rodney, what are we going—"

"It's all over the news," Rodney finally says. "The fight."

"Did they say anything about Farhan?"

"No, nothing about him or Marquese," Rodney says. "There's only one person named. Me."

Jawahir's heart feels as if it jumps from her chest to her throat and stops her ability to speak.

"Don't worry, Larry will help us figure out something," Rodney says, unsure if he believes it.

"But it wasn't your fault! You were protecting me," Jawahir says. It sounds like she's on the verge of tears.

"They'll call it an assault, which violates my parole. I'll go back inside, but I'd rather die—"

"It can't be that bad inside, can it?"

"I didn't finish," Rodney says. "I'd rather die than be separated from you."

15

RODNEY

"That's what happened, honest, Larry."
Rodney's at his uncle's door. Jawahir stands
behind him, clutching onto his left arm. "It
was pure self-defense, you ask anyone who
was there—"

"The brothers will say that, but you think
the Somali kids will say the same thing?"
Larry asks. He looks apologetic like he knows
he probably offended Jawahir.

"Maybe so, but I—we—need a place to

hide, just one night."

Uncle Larry's got the door partially open, but the chain is still on. "Then what?"

Rodney pulls Jawahir closer. "Then we're running away together."

"Where you running to, Poe?"

Rodney turns toward Jawahir, bends down to kiss her, and then returns his attention back to his uncle. "I don't know yet, but someplace where there isn't all this hate."

Larry shakes his head like he's stunned at the words from Rodney's mouth. "You want to act like a man, yet you talk like some kid. There isn't any place in the world like that, Poe."

Rodney looks away from his uncle. "Maybe not, but until we figure it out, can we—"

"Just a second." Larry undoes the chain and opens the door. "Just you, Poe."

Rodney kisses Jawahir. "I'll be right back," he says before stepping in the doorway. He takes six steps inside. His uncle wears his blue uniform from his job driving a shuttle back and forth over the same roads every day. Rodney wonders if a job like that isn't much different than prison or his time at CHS. Nothing but doing the same things someone tells you to do over and over as you count minutes, hours, and days until it's done. His uncle even wears an ugly blue shirt like Rodney did at CHS.

"Listen, one night, but that's it," Larry says. "I'm not on parole anymore, but I don't need any light on me harboring you. If you get caught, I don't know anything. You didn't see me."

Rodney nods. "She's staying with me. Do you think you could—"

His uncle finishes his sentence with a smile. "Find another place to be? No problem, but don't be getting busy on my bed. The couch is foldout, and there are some sheets in the bathroom closet."

"I didn't really plan, so . . ." Rodney averts his eyes, embarrassed.

Larry roars in laughter and slaps his nephew's back. "Top drawer of the dresser by the bed."

16

JAWAHIR

"Is the sun really rising already?" Jawahir sighs sadly. She rises from the sofa bed, the thin sheet wrapped around her bare shoulders. "I don't want our night to end."

Rodney pulls her gently back next to him. "Who says it has to?"

Jawahir strokes the side of Rodney's unshaven face. "What are we going to do?"

"You have any relatives we could—" Rodney starts.

"No, most of them live here in Minnesota, but I'm sure those who don't wouldn't allow me to live with them. If so, it would only be to trick me until they could send me back to my father."

"I got a cousin in Chicago, one of Larry's sons. Maybe—"

"My father would find us," Jawahir whispers. "He would spare no expense. I'm sure right now he has all of his and Farhan's father's friends out looking for me as if I were some criminal."

"You're not a criminal, nor am I," Rodney reassures. Jawahir kisses him. "I was, but I'm not now."

"I don't care about anything before we met. All I care about is since you helped me that—"

Rodney laughs. He points at her dress and his shirt on the floor. Both stained with blood from the fight. "It seems like we're trapped in some sort of circle."

Jawahir pulls closer. "Life is a circle. I'm just glad we're traveling around it together."

Rodney takes a deep breath and reaches for

his phone. He scrolls through his messages, but stops suddenly. "I've got a bunch of calls from my PO. I gotta get out of town. Jump on the bus, and quick."

"I'll come with you."

"No, not now. You go back home and tell everyone it's over between us. Renounce me, do whatever you have to do so you don't get punished or hurt. Save yourself. Then once I got things squared in Chicago, I'll send for you, through Larry, and we'll leave all this behind."

"I don't think I can—" Jawahir starts, but Rodney silences her with a kiss.

"We went too many years without knowing each other. We can make it a few more—"

"Days, not weeks." She senses a day without Rodney will feel like the longest week of the year.

17

"I promise, days, not weeks." Rodney leans out of bed and reaches for his pants. He pulls a roll of bills from his pants pocket.

"Look, buy a disposable phone." Rodney hands Jawahir money. "Hide it from everyone, but use it to call me. I'll go crazy not hearing your voice."

"Sit backward on the bus, so it seems real."

Rodney laughs. He's starting to speak when his phone rings. It's Larry. He picks up.

"Uncle Larry, I need to get a hold of Drayton in Chicago. I lost his number. Can you hook me up?"

"Why? You thinking of staying with him?" Larry asks over a noisy background.

"Just until I can get things sorted out," Rodney says.

"It's best. I mean, it is all over the news. They got the mayor, the police, a whole bunch of preachers and whatever, appealing for peace. They closed your school for the day. Crazy, man."

"They say anything more about me or how Marquese is doing?"

"No, just that a lot of people are still in the hospital, and they're looking for you," Larry says. "Even showed your photo. Don't worry. It's one from your yearbook, not some ugly mug shot."

"I'm not turning myself in. I didn't do anything wrong, but nobody is going to listen."

"They can't listen because there's too much noise," Larry says. "People only hear what they want to hear, that's the whole problem.

People got to walk around in somebody else's shoes."

"I know. I didn't used to get that, but I learned that at CHS. Empathy. But people judge."

"That's the truth, and sooner or later you're gonna face it, but I understand you needing to get out of town, getting some time and distance. That's the best strategy. You need money or anything?"

Rodney puts the phone against his bare chest. "He wants to know if we need anything?" he asks Jawahir. She drops the sheet from her bare shoulders, and Rodney smiles wide. "Yeah, another hour here."

18

"Get in the van!" Jawahir's father shouts at her. Shouting has been his normal tone since she returned home this morning. "You're going to the hospital to visit Farhan. You will visit him every day until—"

"Father, I am sorry about everything," Jawahir says, cutting her dad off. Even though she did exactly as Rodney suggested— denounced him and vowed never even to speak his name again—her father is not satisfied. She might as well be speechless for he refuses to listen to anything she says.

"I don't believe you," he counters as she climbs in. Ayaan follows behind. The front seat remains empty since her mother is working, and it's like her father doesn't want to be that close to Jawahir, like she caught a disease or something. "I believe your actions have brought shame on your family and on your community. I want to hear nothing more, understood?"

"Yes, Father," Jawahir whispers. The ride to the hospital is mostly silent, as if her father is too angry, feels too betrayed, to talk with anyone. I know betrayal, too, Jawahir thinks as she glares at Ayaan, sitting next to her. Ayaan, who obviously betrayed her and set all of these horrible actions in motion.

At the hospital, her father drops them by the front door and goes to park the van. "I know what room he is in," Ayaan boasts, like she knows the answer to some test. Ayaan, with longer legs and greater eagerness to see Farhan, races ahead. Jawahir catches up just as the elevator door is closing. Rather than pushing a floor, Ayaan holds the door close button.

"I don't believe you either." Her voice is cutting, like a scalpel or Farhan's switchblade.

"I'm telling the truth," Jawahir lies. She starts to repeat her story about how wrong she was to take up with Rodney. How she knows now that everyone else was right and she was wrong. As she says the words, she tries to make them real, but Ayaan knows her too well.

"Where is he?" Ayaan demands.

"I don't know."

"He's dead."

Jawahir tries to keep her hands steady. "How could you say that?"

"That's what you'd better believe, Jawahir, because he's never coming back to you." Jawahir starts to cry. "And you blew your chance with Farhan after what that thug did to him."

"Rodney's not a thug."

Ayaan pushes herself toward Jawahir. "You tell us you want nothing to do with it and it was all a mistake, yet you still defend him. He took from you the ability to tell the truth. You didn't come home last night, so I have to wonder what else he took from you."

Jawahir thinks about slapping Ayaan, but holds back. She feels no shame, no regret for what happened last night with Rodney. Her love is bigger than her faith.

Ayaan lets go of the button and the elevator begins to rise. As they pass by each floor, Ayaan continues to bad-mouth not just Rodney, but all the African American kids at Northeast. "Rodney belongs behind bars. They should never have let him out."

Ayaan steps of the elevator, but Jawahir doesn't move. When she reaches to press the close button, Ayaan yanks her from the elevator, then down the hall. She lets go as they enter Farhan's room. Jawahir feels like fainting from the sight of Farhan's face covered with bandages and the tubes in his arms.

Farhan motions for just Jawahir to come closer. She stands next to the bed. "I'm sorry about all of this, Farhan. This has gone too far. You've got to stop. Mercy. Peace."

Farhan takes Jawahir's hand and pulls her closer. "I'm sorry about your dress."

Jawahir's shaken. *That is what you're sorry about?* she thinks. *My dress, not stabbing someone?*

"When I get out of here, I will buy you a new one," Farhan speaks through clenched teeth, his jaw probably broken during the fight. "In fact, I'll buy you two new dresses, Jawahir. A white one for you to wear to our wedding. And a black one for you to wear to Rodney's funeral."

RODNEY

"There are three things worth killing for," Marquese tells Rodney. Rodney rides in the big blue MegaBus on the way to Chicago; Marquese is still in the big white hospital on the way to recovery. "I guess you don't think about something like that until something like this."

Rodney tries apologizing again, but Marquese isn't having it. "It's worth dying for your family, and your family is all your brothers, and that includes you. It's worth dying for your country, and . . ."

Rodney tries to hear over his rumbling stomach. The money he gave Jawahir for a phone and the one-way ticket to Chicago was almost all the money he had. "So what's the third, Marquese?"

"Your woman. I didn't get that because you know I ain't never had nothing like you and Jawahir. Man, I can see it between you. You two are like cartoon magnets with wiggly lines drawing you to each other. I think that's why I stood up. Farhan wasn't just insulting me, you, and all brothers. He was insulting love, and that's just wrong. When I'm dead and gone, all that money I made ain't gonna remember me. It ain't gonna cry; it's just going into somebody else's pocket. But you, you got it."

"Had it." Rodney tells Marquese about going to Chicago and being away from Jawahir. "I could come in the hospital with you and they could cut out a piece of me, and it won't hurt more than this."

"Then why you running?"

"If I stay, I'm going to get violated," Rodney confesses. "I can't go back inside."

"You afraid Jawahir would pull an Aaliyah and drop you when you're—"

"No, that's not it." Of this, Rodney is more than one hundred percent sure. "But I said I wasn't going back in. I told everybody at CHS, everybody at home, and everybody at school that I was done with that life. But mostly, I told myself that I'd never step foot inside again and I'm going to keep my word."

"I'll testify that you were trying to break up the fight." Rodney flashes not on the images of the fight, but the sound of the knife entering Marquese's body and then his body hitting the ground. "I'll tell—"

"And we know how much judges and POs believe what young black men say," Rodney says, feeling his anger rise. "Farhan and his buddies got way more cred than any of us and you know that."

Marquese, who loves to argue, doesn't say a word. Both he and Rodney know the system. "So how you feeling?" Rodney asks.

"When you going home and going back to school?"

Marquese laughs, then starts coughing. When he starts talking again, his tone is different, like he's in pain. "I don't think school will take me back. I think they want me gone, and you too I bet."

"Probably, that's what they do." Rodney remembers Principal Evans trying to get him to enroll in River Creek Academy, one of the charter schools the district uses to warehouse problem kids and ex-cons. But since he wanted to play football, or thought he did, he got Bryant to get Coach to convince Evans to let him back in. He's got no ally in his corner now, and more enemies than he's ever had.

Marquese and Rodney keep talking; it makes the miles so much quicker, and Rodney can only assume it makes hours laying in hospital bed a little less painful by talking to a friend.

Rodney finally ends the call when another comes in: Jawahir. "It's her, Marquese, I gotta go."

"Family, country, and love," Marquese says. "Worth killing for, worth dying for."

Rodney smiles at the idea of big bad Marquese falling in love.

He quits smiling when Jawahir tells him what Farhan said about buying two dresses.

"I'm scared, Rodney," she says. Rodney hears the terror in her voice. He balls his fists in rage.

"Gimme a couple of days and—"

"It won't make a difference," Jawahir says, her voice still shaking. "Nothing will make a difference. We'll never be together, not in Chicago, not here, maybe not until we get to Jannah."

"Jannah?" Rodney asks.

"Paradise, or what you might think of as heaven."

Rodney tries to hold back a laugh, but can't manage to do so. "I ain't going to Paradise."

"How can you say that?"

"Heaven's for good people, and I've only been a good person since I met you."

Silence makes Rodney think the phone's

cut out, but when he looks at the screen, the call seems to be working. "Jawahir, are you there?"

"Yes, Rodney, yes, I am here. I'll pray for you, for both of us to go to Paradise."

"Jawahir, when we're together again," Rodney whispers softly as if Jawahir's ear was next to his, "that's heaven for me."

20

JAWAHIR

"You can't sit here," ZamZam says sharply as Jawahir tries to sit at the table filled with other ninth-grade Somali girls. Girls she's known most of her life, girls she thought were her friends. "Nobody wants you at this table. Nobody wants you at this school. Why don't you and Rodney do all of us a favor and take your disgusting little love affair someplace where we don't have to watch."

Jawahir pulls a deep breath into her

lungs, shuts her mouth tight, and heads for another table.

With the same response.

And another, and another, and another until she's exhausted half of the tables occupied by Somali students. She looks quickly over at the tables occupied by the African American students. The one closest contains the girls who were about to jump her when she was down, if not for Rodney.

Humiliated, she turns and dumps her lunch into the garbage. Trying not to cry, she walks head down out of the cafeteria, but once she's outside, she breaks into a run.

As she's running down the hallway, she hears a voice yell her name over and over. She collects herself, turns, and sees Principal Evans standing, looking very much pissed off. "Jawahir, in my office, now." Evans motions for Jawahir to follow her like she was a scared pet dog.

Jawahir's stomach clenches with fear; she's never been in a principal's office. Never been in trouble, never been anything but an A student and obedient child with lots of friends. Now she's lost all of those things, and the reason she lost them—Rodney—isn't anywhere close.

"You can't run in the hallways," Evans scolds after Jawahir steps inside the doorway.

Jawahir nods but thinks it's odd Evans called her in to say that. *What am I doing here?* she thinks.

"Now, Jawahir, as you know we've had a few little issues recently between different groups of students." Despite feeling terrible, Jawahir feels like laughing at Evans describing brawls, a stabbing, and multiple arrests as "a few little issues." Evans continues, "I brought together a small group with some outside help, but basically, that doesn't seem to be working. So what I'm thinking, and I think Coach Martin might agree with me: go big, go long."

Jawahir nods but says nothing. All she knows about football is that Martin coaches it.

"I understand that you and Rodney Marshall have become quite close, actually. A couple, I understand, is that correct?"

Jawahir shakes her head to the negative. "We were, but that's over." It hurts her to tell the lie, as if it might jinx their love and that somehow by saying those words it might make them true.

Evans fiddles with items on her desk. "Really? I must have had some incorrect information."

She knows she shouldn't, but Jawahir asks anyway. "Why does that matter?"

"Like I said, go big, go long. As you know, homecoming is almost upon us, and I think you and Rodney as a couple could be a symbol of these two groups coming together. Everyone would see that it is possible for people to overcome their prejudices when they get to know each other as people. Agree?"

Jawahir nods again. "But like I said, that's over between us."

Evans shakes her head back and forth, sighing but saying nothing. "Then who were you texting on your cell phone during first period? And second period? Do I need to go on?"

"Nobody." Did a teacher see her or was it Ayaan snitching on her again?

"Well, if you should happen to text this person you say you broke up with, you can tell him that I gathered enough information about what happened with Farhan to convince his PO to leave him alone. And you can also tell him that if he agrees to my plan, then I'll talk to his PO, and I'll let him back in my school. If not, then not."

"You can't do that!"

"Actually I can."

Jawahir starts to speak, but realizes her words mean nothing to Evans.

"I'd hurry up about it," Evans says. "Homecoming is on Friday. Basically, Jawahir, the clock is ticking."

Jawahir turns from Evans and stares at the clock on the wall. Never has time moved more slowly than now; never did it move so quickly as the night she spent with Rodney.

"You're dismissed."

After leaving Evans' office, Jawahir heads not for her next class, but for the light rail. She'll finish up her few precious phone minutes talking to Rodney, pretending he is sitting behind her on the train as she whispers, "Rodney, I love you, please come back to me because my life is broken and only you can fix it."

21

RODNEY

"Welcome back, Rodney," Principal Evans
says in a voice way too upbeat for the events
of the day. Rodney had borrowed money from
his cousin and boarded the train the day he
got Jawahir's phone call. His first day back
at school was marked by a near fight in every
class, if not between him and one of the Somali
students, then between one of his friends and
one of Farhan's friends.

Rodney tries to smile, but can't make

himself do so until he drops his hand from his lap and Jawahir, sitting next to him, catches it in her hand. "I don't know what you want me to say, Principal Evans."

Principal Evans points at their intertwined hands. "You don't need to say a word. Most communication is nonverbal, and that right there is the symbol that this school needs to heal."

The students in the "healing group"— almost all girls—nod in agreement. Reverend Cook tells a parable about the power of symbols, followed by Shaykh Abdi Abdallah relating a similar tale. Rodney scratches his head as these wise men of God try to out-do one another like two twelve-year-olds.

Once they are finished, Principal Evans opens up the discussion about the importance of Rodney and Jawahir attending the homecoming dance. She makes a big show out of handing them their tickets.

"I guess the next dress you're going to buy won't be for my funeral," Rodney jokes, but Jawahir doesn't laugh. Rodney looks at her and sees the color drain from her face. She releases Rodney's hand from hers.

"Daughter, is that him?" an older Somali man shouts at Jawahir from the open doorway. "I said, is that him?"

Jawahir stands and puts herself in front of Rodney. The man screams obscenities at him. Shaykh Abdi Abdallah tries to calm the man down, but with little success. The Somali students in the group rise from their chairs and move away from the men. Shouting, mostly in Somali but with mixed in English words, the men stand toe to toe.

The lone security guard, a young African American man, speaks into his radio and then tries to get between the two men, grabbing at Jawahir's dad's coat. "Don't touch me!" Jawahir's father pulls away from the guard.

"Sir, please, if you'd just step out into my office," Evans says, her voice shaking. "I will explain how I believe your daughter's bravery is going to change the school climate for the better!"

This sets him off more. He shouts threats

at Principal Evans. The meeting ends when a security team arrives. Jawahir's father resists, even punching the black officer, until he's maced and subdued.

JAWAHIR

"I forbid this!" Jawahir's father stands blocking the front door. His arms are crossed, his eyes glaring at his daughter. Rodney's outside in the back of a rented car that Larry is driving.

"You promised!" she shouts. Then Jawahir reminds her father that in return for the school not pressing charges for his assault on the school security officer, he agreed to let Jawahir attend the dance.

Jawahir's mom is upstairs with Jawahir's younger brothers to protect them from watching this scene: the site of a humbled father isn't something, Jawahir knows, that her parents want their sons to see.

"Would you rather spend the night in jail?" Jawahir asks.

"You mean like Rodney has?"

Jawahir doesn't answer. Her father doesn't know that, he just assumes the worst. Always has and always will. One minute, Jawahir believes that she and Rodney can be the healing symbol that Principals Evans wants, but at times like now, she knows there's no chance. The wound is too deep. It needs, as Rodney said, time and distance, neither which seems possible.

"If you don't move, Father, I will call the police to have you arrested," Jawahir says as calmly as she can even though her knees are shaking. "I was a witness. I will testify against you. Gladly."

"You don't have a phone to call—"

Jawahir produces the phone from under

her dress. He doesn't know all the minutes are gone.

"Fine, go to your dance, daughter, but know that you will be alone."

"No, Rodney will be with me. You can't stop us—"

"I have talked to the other fathers. They are not allowing their children to attend. You will be all alone in the world. You should get used to that feeling. He will leave you, like all of them leave their families. You think he is special because he looks at you, because he kisses you, because—"

"We're in love, Father!"

When Jawahir reaches the car, her cheek is bright red from the force of her father's hand striking her face.

RODNEY

"This is very disappointing," Principal Evans says to Rodney and Jawahir. Not only have most of the Somali students boycotted the dance, a good number of African American ones have as well.

"Maybe they'll show up later," Rodney says over his shoulder as Evans leaves the table. In the nearly empty gym, Rodney and Jawahir hold hands and kiss like any other homecoming couple.

"Rodney, a second," Bryant says. Bryant hasn't said a word to Rodney since the fight. Rodney tenses, tries to figure out what Bryant might want, not liking any of the possibilities.

"Busy."

"It's important, bro."

"Then tell me now."

"It's private," Bryant whispers. "It's not about her."

"There's no her, Bryant. There's an us. What we've been through, what we've still got to go through, that unites people. It's not like being on a team losing a few games, this is serious stuff."

"Fine." Bryant pulls a chair out and sits down. He smiles at Jawahir, but Rodney doesn't think it's sincere. "I just wanted to let you know that most of us, well, we're still not down with this, but—"

"It doesn't matter what you think." Rodney quickly recalls all the times in the past he wishes he would've said that, felt that way, and not followed the crowd onto the street and in harm's way.

"You should know it's all good. Everybody likes how you stood up for Marquese. How you took—"

Rodney cuts him off, worried about the next words out of his mouth. "Enough, Bryant!"

"I just want to say, we got your back if you should—" It is as far as Bryant gets before he, Rodney, and Jawahir turn toward a huge commotion. The door to the gym bursts open as a group of Farhan's friends pour into the gym wielding baseball bats and metal pipes.

"Let's go!" Jawahir shouts, but Rodney motions for her to get under the table. He rips off his jacket, picks up the metal chair on which he'd been sitting, and charges into the middle of the melee.

JAWAHIR

Jawahir prays, as she always does, for the
violence to end, but never has it been so close,
so loud, so real.

Jawahir waits under the table, closing her
eyes against the awful sounds, until she feels
Rodney's hand grab hers. "Let's go!" Rodney
shouts. She crawls out shaking, but starts
crying when she sees Rodney's condition.
His head is bleeding, as is his chest. His shirt
is ripped wide open, while his pants have a

huge hole in the right leg that blood pours far too quickly.

Jawahir looks past Rodney to see the carnage of wounded warriors behind him.

"Now!"

Jawahir scrambles to her feet, but before leaving with Rodney she grabs the tablecloth. As they run for the exit—Rodney more limping than running—Jawahir tries to rip the cloth into bandages. They exit the gym through a side door into the school. Like that first day they kissed, they announce themselves by opening a security door. The sirens of the door can't match those of the police cars and ambulances Rodney hears pulling up in front of the school. The flashing lights color the night as red as the blood spilled on the gym floor.

"What are we doing to do?" Jawahir asks.

Rodney motions for her to sit with him against the wall. "I'll call Larry to come get us."

"You should go to a hospital," Jawahir begs.

Rodney shakes his head. "No, they ask too many questions."

Jawahir starts wiping away the blood from Rodney's face. "What did you do?"

Rodney says nothing. He just breathes heavy and lets Jawahir attend to him. She wraps a makeshift bandage around his forehead. She reaches for his hurt leg, but he pulls away in pain. "I'm fine."

"Let me see it."

Rodney rolls his pants up. A massive bleeding gash runs from his ankle to his knee. As Jawahir does her best to stop the bleeding, Rodney's on his phone with Larry. They speak quickly, mostly Rodney agreeing to whatever Larry says to him. "He'll meet us a couple blocks away. We've got to go."

"Can you walk a few blocks?"

"What, you won't carry me?" Rodney cracks, but Jawahir's too scared to laugh or smile. "Look, tonight I'll lean on you and another night, you'll lean on me. And we'll do that—"

"Forever." Jawahir helps Rodney to his feet and helps him stand, then walk. "And ever."

RODNEY

"You should've listened to me, Poe. I told you this was a mistake," Larry says. Rodney's sprawled on his back in the small apartment. Larry's cleaning the wound on his leg, while Jawahir works on the multiple cuts on his face and neck. "No offense, Jawahir, but I got to look out for my own."

"That's the problem," Jawahir says. "We're all God's own. We're all riders on the same train."

"Maybe," Larry grunts. "What the hell happened in there?"

Rodney answers part of the question, what happened to him, but he won't answer all of it. He won't tell Larry or Jawahir what he did, which was simple: whatever it took to protect Jawahir.

"So what are you going to do?" Larry asks. Rodney wishes his uncle would stop asking questions that he has no idea how to answer. Jawahir starts to answer for Rodney, but Larry cuts her off. "Again, no offense, but you're fourteen, maybe fifteen, so how can you know anything?"

Jawahir nods and goes back to cleaning the nasty cut across Rodney's nose.

"I'm almost forty and I can tell you how the world works, and it's not like that. I know when you're young, you gotta believe the world is a place where everything works out, but it doesn't. It's the opposite. I'm a grown man with a college degree, but the only history I get to know is that of the same streets I travel over and over again, driving that stupid van for no money while wearing a uniform uglier than the one in Stillwater."

"Larry, cool it," Rodney says.

"No, listen. You two had better cool it, because this time people got hurt, next time people might die. Do you hear what I'm saying? Is this love you think you have worth people dying for?"

Rodney sits up and smiles through his busted-up lips at Jawahir. "Yes, Uncle Larry, yes it is."

Larry shakes his head first like he's disgusted but then a grin breaks out on his face. "Good one, Poe. That's like you, an endless romantic willing to do anything in the name of truth, love, and beauty."

Rodney wipes the blood, someone else's probably, from his hands and then as gentle as the night was violent, places them softly on Jawahir's shoulders. "She is truth, love, and beauty."

Jawahir lays her head against Rodney's bruised right hand. "He is truth, love, and beauty."

"I'd tell you to get a room, but you already got one," Larry cracks. "Mine."

"Last night here, I promise," Rodney says.

Larry finishes applying the bandage to Rodney's leg. "I'll find someplace else—"

"No, I think we're going to be up all night talking," Rodney says. "This is too hard. We have to figure out what to do. I got to use those CBT skills I learned at CHS. Get away from the negative and—"

"Rodney, I don't see a win here." Larry stands and starts to walk toward his bedroom.

"What do you mean, Larry?" Rodney asks.

"Do you think suddenly everything's going to be okay?" Larry reaches into his shirt pocket, pulls out a smoke, and lights it. As the embers burn, Rodney remembers Larry comparing love to fire, that as long as there is fuel there is fire. He can't imagine ever running out of fuel for Jawahir.

Rodney doesn't answer.

Larry reaches for the light switch. "I'm sorry, but it seems to me that your love is hopeless."

"No!" Jawahir cries. "Our love is endless!"

Rodney motions for Jawahir to lie next to him. "You're both right and wrong. Larry, I know you think we're just stupid kids in love, but we're smart. We know our love is hopeless. But you know what? If you could feel what I feel, you'd know she's right: our hearts tell us our love is endless."

Larry flicks off the light and heads toward his room. "So I guess that's the real question. All this other stuff is just smoke. You got to get to the source, Poe. What's stronger: the heart or the mind?"

JAWAHIR

"Back to back," Jawahir whispers as they board the northbound train. They had answered Larry's questions through the night and into dawn on the sofa bed in Larry's apartment.

"It's only three stops, then we change trains and head back south," Rodney whispers. Like the first time they rode the train to talk, Jawahir holds a book in front of her face while Rodney pretends to talk into his phone. But it's early Saturday morning, and the train is mostly empty except for a few mothers with young children and older men reading newspapers. No one notices them; no one knows them.

"I wish we could ride this train forever," Jawahir says. "Talking like this. No one bothering us."

"Me too, but we can't, we know that. Like we talked about last night, every train ends up someplace, but we don't have anywhere to go. We've got no money, no relatives who will shelter us, and no place that will accept us. We're a nation of two exiled from the world."

"I like that, Rodney, but I'd like to think of us as two people on a sinking ship who know enough to get off. We get on a life raft and just drift and drift endlessly until the end of time."

The train jolts at the American Boulevard station, the one just before the train heads into the tunnel for the airport stops. Jawahir faces the tunnel like a drowning woman would stare at a life vest.

The train's extra noisy in the tunnel, so they exchange no words, which is fine with Jawahir. All the words have been said, all the options considered, and Larry's question of heart and mind answered.

A few TSA and MSP workers get on and off at the Terminal 2 station, but even more enter and exit at Terminal 1. Jawahir and Rodney join the exit and move to the other side of the track. They hold hands, swinging them back and forth, like some old grandfather clock. Time is ticking down. The southbound train comes into the station. They get on and sit next to each other, laughing nervously about nothing as the train picks up speed. It heads back to Terminal 2 and then exits into daylight. Just before they leave the tunnel, Jawahir points to the timetable of the next trains. "North or south?" she asks.

"Like heaven, north is up, so north." Rodney checks the timetable and his phone, and they exit.

Hand in hand they walk from the stop up 34th Avenue, not saying a word. In the distance, they hear no alarm of an exit door kicked open, no police car arriving, no ambulance pulling away. Nothing but the lonesome whistle of the metro train. *I will never be lonesome or alone again*, Jawahir thinks.

As the train makes the stop at American Boulevard, the last stop before entering the airport tunnel, Jawahir climbs over the fence first and then helps Rodney scale the metal barrier.

"Our love is hopeless," Rodney points at his head.

"No, our love is endless." Jawahir puts a hand over her heart.

"It is both," Rodney reminds her, and she nods.

"I love you Rodney—"

"I love you Jawahir, now and—"

"Forever," they say together as they stare into in each other's eyes, no longer talking back to back. Beneath them, the rumble of the train shakes the bridge they stand on, like a tiny earthquake. Cars pass by, planes fly over, and the train rolls on as people of every color get on with their lives, except Rodney and Jawahir, who join hands and jump from the top of the tunnel into the path of the speeding oncoming train.

ABOUT THE AUTHOR

Patrick Jones is the author of more than twenty novels for teens. He has also written two nonfiction books about combat sports, *The Main Event*, on professional wrestling, and *Ultimate Fighting*, on mixed martial arts. He has spoken to students at more than one hundred alternative schools, including residents of juvenile correctional facilities. Find him on the web at www.connectingya.com and on Twitter: @PatrickJonesYA.